Frank Roe Batchelder

Roses for Mabel

Lyrics and Musings

Frank Roe Batchelder

Roses for Mabel
Lyrics and Musings

ISBN/EAN: 9783744788434

Printed in Europe, USA, Canada, Australia, Japan

Cover: Foto ©Andreas Hilbeck / pixelio.de

More available books at **www.hansebooks.com**

BY

FRANK ROE BATCHELDER

"

"I give you the roses of love," said he.
Louise Chandler Moulton.

WORCESTER

PRINTED PRIVATELY

MDCCCXCI

The Author's Private Press.

THE DEDICATION.

TO MABEL,

_to whose love and gentle influence I owe my noblest
thoughts, my loftiest ideals, my manliest endeavors,
and in whose companionship the happiest days
of my life have been spent, I send this little
book, to speak for me the countless loving thoughts that well up in my
heart and go forth to her, finding her out, wherever
she may be._

CONTENTS.

THE MINSTREL AFIELD.

I shall never, in the years remaining,
Paint you pictures, no, nor carve you statues,
Make you music that should all express me;
So it seems: I stand on my attainment;
This of verse alone one life allows me;
Verse and nothing else have I to give you.
Other heights in other lives, God willing—
All the gifts from all the heights, your own, Love!

Yet a semblance of resource avails us—
Shade so finely touched, love's sense must seize it.
Take these lines, look lovingly and nearly,
Lines I write the first time and the last time.

Take and keep my fifty poems finished;
Where my heart lies, let my brain lie also.

Oh, their Rafael of the dear Madonnas,
Oh, their Dante of the dread Inferno,
Wrote one song—and in my brain I sing it,
Drew one angel—borne, see, on my bosom!

BROWNING: One Word More.

MABEL.

Beating heart! we come again
Where my love reposes :
This is Mabel's window-pane ;
These are Mabel's roses.

FREDERICK LOCKER :
At Her Window.

ROSES FOR MABEL.

MABEL'S EASTER ROSES.

R ADIANT morning, blessed Easter, day that
comest as of old,
Bringing still the wondrous promise that the Resurrection told,
Thou shalt hear again the music that our lips have
learned to sing,
And the prayers that rise like incense unto Christ,
our Lord and King.

Earth shall wake and catch the impulse of the
Resurrection song ;
Nature, joining in the chorus, shall the praise of
men prolong ;
Birds and brooks and flowers shall hear it, and
from dumbness summon voice,
Till the least of God's creations finds a reason to
rejoice.

Easter roses, truant children of the summer that
we lost,
Ye have lingered, finding sunshine, never fearful of
the frost ;

There is one who loves your perfume, one who
loves the Christ that died :
Go to her, ye roses, carry blessings of the Easter-
tide.

Spread your perfume round about her; bid her
happiness increase ;
Let the heart that never falters know a never-
failing peace ;
She hath followed in His footsteps who for us was
sacrificed ;
Easter morn shall bring her nearer, nearer to the
blessed Christ.

MANHOOD.

I.—AT THE PORTAL.

DAY so long looked for, thou art here at last,
     And boyhood's midnight trembles on the
          chime ;
Push back the curtains of my soul, O Time,
That I may have one long look at the past,
With all its joys and sorrows, ere I cast
     My eyes on heights which yet remain to climb,
     And take my staff, and murmur out a rhyme,
And wipe away the tear-drops coming fast.

Tears now? Aye, all the heart's great wealth of
          tears,—
     Tears for the good that has been thrown away.—
Tears for the squandering of golden years,—
     Tears for the pure love that I lost one day,—
Tears for the careless words, the foolish fears,
     And things unsaid which it was mine to say.

II.—SORROW.

Sorrow hath dwelt with me not over long,
     And yet, how changed the tenor of my days !
     Sorrow that cut my heart as the knife flays,
And yet a sorrow fit to make me strong,

Quickening the dead soul that had died in wrong,
  And raising it in honor, to the praise
  Of the wise God, whose ways are not our ways—
Who finds some good where evils thickest throng.

And the dear friends—God bless them, every one ;
  First in my heart and first in all my good,
She who hath taught me all save truth to shun,
  She who could read each varying thought and
      mood,
And left no prayer unsaid, no work undone,
  Which might attest her joy in motherhood.

III.—MY LOST LOVE.

And you, belovëd? This day was to be
  Our gladdest day.   Alas, we sit apart ;
  The old love burns undying in my heart ;
And in yours—ah, therein I may not see.
Pity you have, perhaps, in some degree,—
  You were so gentle—tender without art,—
  And though no tears to mine responsive start,
Your happiness is happiness to me.

Something my life lacks, which had made it great,
  And yet my life may therefore be more true ;
Today I enter in at the new gate,
  Not proud and glad, but thinking, dear, of you,
Not finding glory, now, in man's estate,
  But humbly meek, and with my heart in rue.

TO THEE, BELOVED. . .

I SEEM to see your little room,
   And. from it looking down,
A face that once dispelled my gloom,
   And for me wore no frown.
There from your window looking out,
   I wonder if you see
The snow still lying round about,
   And no leaf on the tree.

We walked, once, in the garden there,
   Adown the leafy aisle ;
No spot on earth was then more fair,
   Since then I had your smile ;
But you on Massachusetts hills
   Today behold the sun,
And here a songbird comes and trills
   For me in Washington.

Yet here, as there, still comes the day
    When Love shall rule the heart,
The rich shall smile, the poor be gay,
    And tears forget to start.
'T is Christmas-tide the whole land through,
    Amid New England's snows,
Or here where the Potomac blue
    Down to the great sea flows.

And Christmas brings that other time
    When I shall think of you.
(Ah, if the tears be in my rhyme,
    It need not ring less true !)
One more rose blossomed—one more year
    For womanhood to show.
God bless you !   If it 's brought you cheer,
    Thank God it could be so.

I send you roses from the South,—
    A book for silent hours,—
Sweet words from a good woman's mouth,—
    The sweetest of the flowers ;
And keep the book for Friendship's sake,
    If you will have no more,
Though all the love you will not take
    Be lying at your door.

But O my roses, you shall go
　To speak my message clear :
I love her ; oh, I love her so !
　Though she so cold appear.
Go, make her tender heart to stir ;
　Whatever Friendship 's done,
'T is only Love would send to her
　Roses from Washington !

ZEPHYR AND SHADOW.

A SOFT wind came from the dreamy south,
    And opened the blushing rose ;
It brought a warm rain after the drouth,
    The violets to unclose ;
And the morn seemed brighter, and earth more
        blest,
    Because of the opening flowers,
Till the south-wind failed, and the wind blew west,
    And the drouth drank up the showers.

When my lady woke and greeted the day,
    Her cheeks bloomed fair like the rose,
And her tender eyes, in their own sweet way,
    Had the hue the violet knows ;
And life grew brighter, and full of glee,
    And my heart leaped at her call ;
Oh, queen among women—the dearest, she,
    And the fairest of them all !

But the smile grew fainter and left her lips,
　　And the love-light left her eyes ;
The magic touch of her finger-tips
　　Died out as the southwind dies ;
The twilight came, for a little space,
　　And the dear dream lingered on,
Till the shadows shut me out from the place,
　　And I looked—and she was gone !

THE ROSE AND THE HANDKERCHIEF.

THEY keep close watch, together,
    Over my weary heart ;
One from the soul of Nature,
    One from the hand of Art.

Did it grow in the garden—
    This she wore on her breast—
Where we once picked the roses,
    Where her love she confessed?

Late it lay on her bosom,
    Reaching a happy goal ;
White were its dainty petals—
    Pure as her own white soul.

Day by day it has withered,
    Fading with every dawn,
But though the leaves are crisping,
    Its sweetness is not gone.

Round about it, the other,
　Fair as the fair white bloom,
Wraps the withering blossom
　Into a softened gloom.

Soft are its folds on my fingers ;
　My kiss its soft sheen knows ;
And it hides the sudden teardrops
　Falling over her rose.

In some far eastern country,
　The moth's thread grew, one day ;
Quaint men fashioned the fabric,
　Far, far off in Cathay.

Then from the gentle giver
　It came one day to me,
Sent with a loving greeting
　Over the smiling sea.

Ever a faint, sweet odor
　Its silken folds give out,
Just as her own sweet presence
　Makes Heaven round about.

Souvenirs fondly cherished,
　All my heart-strings ye stir :
One she chose for me only,
　One God fashioned for her.

Since ye are pure as she is,
  Lie here, over my heart;
Teach me too to be holy,—
  Teach me the knightly part.

And ye both shall cheer my spirit,
  Under the chastening rod,
For I believe in Mabel
  As I believe in God.

A HEART-ACHE.

WHAT was the orchestra playing then?
　　Strange, how I happened to hear that
　　strain—
The old, old "Carnival" over again ;
　　But that was not all that brought the pain,
For my eyes swept round the boxes above,
　　And there, as fair as a queen on her throne,
She sat—ah, the One ! my dear lost love,
　　And I was below her, silent, alone.

It was opening night, and the house was filled ;
　　The hum of whisper and laugh rose loud ;
And no one knew how my heart was chilled :
　　I 'd nothing in common with the crowd.
Pleasure?　Ah me, when it seemed so wrong :
　　I should have been there by her side,
And instead, I was all alone in the throng,
　　Wishing again that I might have died.

She was so beautiful !   Oh, that dress,
　Just as she wore it a year ago ;
The very folds that I then could press
　Close to my heart, for I loved her so.
I was so proud of her, too, that night,
　As we passed the people, her arm in mine,
And I drank in out of her blue eyes bright
　The deepest measure of Love's wild wine.

And then last night.   O my tortured heart !
　Can it be that I really merit this?
She was happy with others, and I, apart,
　Would have given my life to regain that bliss—
To look again in her darling eyes,
　And see no shadow of chilling scorn,
But the old glad welcome, the sweet surprise :
　Ah, it is all gone now,—all gone !

But I love her yet : I could die tonight,
　Smiling at Death, if I thought that she
Would care for me, dead, even, as she might,
　Had Fate been a little kinder to me.
She may doubt, she may scorn, she may turn away,
　Though my will is swayed by her lightest breath ;
But whatever she do or think or say,
　I know that my love will last through death.

The play-house is dark and silent now,
　But I never again can enter there
Without a sight of that fair broad brow,
　Those soft blue eyes, and that golden hair.
And kneeling, tonight, as I pray to God,
　I feel that influence in me stir,
And, bending to kiss His smiting rod,
　I pray He may make me more like her.

What of the play? It was like the rest:
　Love and war and a happy end.
Real life is n't always so blessed:
　Sometimes hearts break and never mend;
And mine, do you think it has found relief,
　Though the merciful tears break forth and flow?
Oh, my dear one—she has not seen my grief,
　But I love her, God knows, as she cannot know.

IN A VOLUME OF FREDERICK LOCKER'S POEMS.

MY well-loved poet! Many times
    You 've heard me quote his happy rhymes,
And now I send them here to you,
That you may learn to love them, too.

What has he sung? No selfish grief,
No song of war, no praise of chief,
But music coming from the heart,
Untouched by all the arts of art.

So goes he smiling down the years,
His laughter sometimes dashed with tears,
But with a heart whose tenderness
Is more than this cold world can guess.

I think he would be glad to know
That these sweet rhymes of his will go
To one whose heart is pure in tone—
Whose soul is gentle—as his own.

Simple and kind in every thought,
His power came to him unsought;
Ah, were my own lyre tuned as true,
What rhymes, my dear, I 'd write to you !

WHAT IS LOVE?

WHAT is Love? went the query round.
Slowly each one an answer found.

Love, said the maiden, is a youth,
Pure in his purpose, strong in his truth,
Noble in action, gentle in speech,
Ready to learn or ready to teach,
Full of the hero's spirit and fire,
Regal in manner and in desire,
Straight as Apollo, mild as a dove,—
These are his glories, and this is Love.

Love, said the young man, is a maid,
Fair as the sunset's flush and shade,
White of soul and gentle in mind,
Sharing the griefs of all her kind,   .
Ready to bear the world's sad stress,
Filled with infinite tenderness,
Moved by all that a heart may move,—
These are her beauties, and this is Love.

So I heard them, and in my soul
Something whispered me : Both are wrong ;
Each hath part and neither the whole.
Then the answer I 'd sought so long
Came as a vision, and I heard
This, the diviner law and word.

Love is not human, for life is short,
And Love has never passed from his court ;
Love is wise as the stars are wise ;
Man has only earth-seeing eyes ;
Love has never been touched by death ;
What is life but a moment's breath ?
Love is not youth, for youth must err :
Passions his unstained soul may stir ;
Love is not as a maiden pure :
Even her faith may not endure.
Make Love grand and noble and wise,
Give him a woman's tender guise,
Fashion him as you can or may—
This is not Love, for this is clay.

Deep in my heart, then, the answer stirred ;
This was what in my soul I heard :
Love is a spirit, hid in the clod ;
Love is an angel, and sent of God.

TO ONE IN THE NORTH.

IF overhead our skies are blue,
    And springlike is the air,
I think—I know—I scarcely knew
    How lovely all things were.

The buds are swelling on the trees,
    The cherry and the haw;
Virginia warms our slightest breeze;—
    All this I hardly saw.

And you, my dear, are wrapped in furs,
    And hear the sleigh-bells ring;
The breeze that in the hemlock stirs
    Has little hint of spring.

Snow on the ground; ice on the lake;
    Jack Frost rules all about,
And roses on your cheeks will make,
    Each time you venture out.

And oh, how strange are Fate's strange ways !
    A breeze from that stern clime
Makes merriment from dismal days,
    And sets my life to rhyme.

So beautiful the world seems now !
    And yet, there is no change.
But who need ask the why or how,
    Though it be passing strange ?

The clouds are fleecier in the blue,
    And in my heart there 's June ;
Ah, Love, two little words from you
    Have put all things in tune.

OLD POINT COMFORT,
    February, 1891.

LOVE SAW THE LIKENESS.

STRANGE chance resemblance! Far away
        from her,
  I find her portrait in this public place—
The golden hair, the sweet lines of her face,
The blue eyes which have made my pulses stir.
And yet, my heart begins to make demur:
  Something too stern about the brow I trace,
  And if the figure has her lissome grace,
The lips are not as smiling as they were.

Ah no, my heart! Because my every thought
  Turns home to her, she greets me on all sides.
    But who, then, bears her this strange like-
      ness? Ah,
How in like mould are good and evil wrought!—
  Clenched in the small, firm hand the skirt half
    hides,
    Behold the knife wherewith was slain Marat!

MY PLAYFUL PUSS.

"My lot she is a kitten,
And my heart's a ball of string."

AH, how those solemn churls
   Who fancy strait-laced girls,
      Would stare—the noodles !—
To see her frisk about,
And laugh and smile and pout,
      And plague the poodles.

And yet those dancing eyes
Have known swift tears to rise,
      Though no repining
Can make her joy to flee
So far she cannot see
      The "silver lining."

But when her heart is light,
And all the world seems bright,
      She 's full of laughter ;

And, much admiring, I
Stand dutifully by,
   Or follow after.

She fathoms everything,—
My heart 's a ball of string,
   And she 's a kitten ;
But oh, I could not live,
If she should ever give
   Poor me the mitten.

Yet, though to mirth inclined,
She 's good ; her heart is kind,
   And unto others
The darling is not slow
Her sympathy to show :
   She *loves* her "brothers."

She trips the stairs adown,
Robed in her dainty gown
   Of blue-trimmed garnet ;
There ! she has caught her dress
And torn it : what a mess !
   She 'll have to darn it.

My puss, I pray you, be
More grave ; come, trust to me
   Your heart for shelter ;

You 've mirth enough to spare :
May I not with you share,
    Dear Helter-Skelter?

Only one word,—take heed :
Let your heart never need
    Its love to label ;
Leave show upon the shelf ;
Be just your own sweet self,
    My darling Mabel !

LOST-LAND.

WHERE do the little maid's playthings go?—
    Childish treasures dear to her heart,
Dropped and forgotten, unfound, and so
    Making, perhaps, the big tears start.
She looks at me from her wistful eyes
    With faith as deep as they are blue ;
"They must be gone to Lost-Land," she sighs ;
    "Sometime I 'll find 'em, I dess : don't you?"

Where do our happinesses go?—
    Love and pity and faith God-willed,
The tender words that have moved us so,
    Joys departed and fond hopes chilled,
Tears that were shed for us, smiles that shone,
    All the sweetest things that we knew,—
They have gone from us, somehow, surely gone :
    I wonder are they in Lost-Land, too?

Dear little maid, if the faith I see
  In your sweet blue eyes, in your sweet blue eyes,
Might only dwell in my heart with me,
  I think that these clouds of care would rise ;
If old joys wait, and old love endures,
  In the Lost-Land shadows whither they fare,
I will trust my hand, little maid, to yours :
  We will go together and seek them there.

THE NEW CUPID.

THE days are gone when some sweet rhyme
    Sufficed to win a maiden ;
We live not in that olden time
    Which with romance was laden.
Poor literature !   For all its pearls
    No least demand arises ;
There's nought can catch the pretty girls
    Now, like athletic prizes !

Here 's Bertie—she whose tender eyes
    I 've been in verse exalting ;
Tom let her choose and keep a prize
    He won at Yale—for vaulting !
And so she keeps my verses in
    Some dusty drawer or corner,
While at her throat she wears a pin—
    Tom's medal—to adorn her !

And Mabel? When she made "her quilt"
    (O aunts, you 've spoiled your nieces !),
She kept us fellows all atilt
    In skirmishing for "pieces."
The quilt has, now, one tie of nine
    She begged me to present her,
While Jim's "prize badges" were so fine
    They all went in the center.

And thus it is. We 've no redress ;
    These athlete chaps will carry
Our girls all off. Now, I love Jess,
    But Jess—she worships Harry.
Well, what can we expect, poor bards?
    Why, Harry 's some attraction—
His record for the "hundred yards" :
    Ten seconds and a fraction !

PARTNERS.

CHANCE made us partners for the hour,
      And if I played a wretched game,
It was because I lost my power
      When back to me the old days came—
When life and love were both in flower.

Partners we were in those dear days,
      Though now it might seem past belief;
And then we played, as Youth still plays,
      The old opponents, Love and Grief—
Love that illumines, Grief that slays.

Strange partners?   Nay, they are akin;
      You find them ever side by side;
Man seeks the gentler one to win,
      But never separate do they bide;
Grief follows where Love enters in.

And are they fallible, these two?
      Sometimes they seem to fail and lose;

We led them a stern chase, 't is true ;
  But was it, then, a clever ruse,
Which our dim vision saw not through?

Dear gentle maiden, in your eyes
  I looked once more this afternoon ;
There were my fairest, bluest skies—
  There was my soul's delightful June ;
And now, what makes the swift tears rise?

This is the outcome of the game :
  Love passed away and Grief delays.
The first, it seems, we knew by name,
  The second by his grievous ways ;
And after all, whom shall we blame?

Not Love, for Love was more than kind ;
  Love made us better than we were ;
Not Grief, for Grief could never bind
  My heart to turn away from her,—
I still am hers, in heart and mind.

What was it, then, that killed the rose?
  What made me less to her, as now?
Be patient, heart of mine ; she chose :
  I will not ask the why and how ;
I will believe it, dear,—God knows.

LOVE FORSAKEN.

(A RONDEL, AFTER DOBSON.)

CUPID stands with his heart a-swelling,—
Quiver empty, and bow unstrung;
Forth from his eyes the big tears are welling;
The love-song dies on his lips, unsung.

Into his soul a sweet hope had sprung;
Now, of its death, his sorrow is telling:
Cupid stands with his heart a-swelling,—
Quiver empty, and bow unstrung.

His rosy lip trembles, his tender heart 's wrung;
Forth he comes from his old-time dwelling;
For some one other aside he is flung,
And now that he finds to a vain hope he clung,
Cupid stands with his heart a-swelling,—
Quiver empty, and bow unstrung.

OCTOBER.

ACCORDING well with my despondent mood,
Thou comest, mourner of the summer slain,
Bringing us cheerless days of clouds and rain,
And winds that sigh as if in grief subdued ;
Birdless is every forest solitude ;
Stubble replaces fields of golden grain ;
And in my heart joy is replaced by pain.—
Sad month, we have a common brotherhood.

The days grow short ; the nights are cold and still ;
Earlier in the house the lamps are lit ;
Frosts nip the tender plants ; on Leicester hill,
Where late we watched the sunset, bats now flit ;
Yet thou, drear month, art not so sad and chill
As this my heart whose hope has gone from it.

1889.

RECOMPENSE.

ALAS for the loves of our boyhood—how soon
Their silver bells jangle and clash out of tune !
They may teach us the deepest of passions, and yet,
How quickly the dearest of girls can forget !

She was fair, she had tender and beautiful eyes ;
I loved her. Why not? Can we always be wise?
Her conquest was easy ; I worshiped her then
As I knew that I never should worship again.

I lived in her smiles, till the time came to part ;
(I wonder if ever she cared, in her heart?)
Then I lived on the past, till I could not deny
That her friendship had ceased when she bade me
good-bye.

.   .   .   .   .   .

It is past : we can never that friendship renew ;
I still have her picture, a keepsake or two,

Which I cherish, as all that is left me, forsooth,
From the wreck of the beautiful dream of my youth.

Today I have seen her !   She came down the street,
Who once might have trampled my heart 'neath her
        feet.
She is changed, yet I saw but the sweet, tender girl
Who years ago set my young heart in a whirl.

I thought of the day when she bade me good-bye,
And smiled as I caught myself stifling a sigh ;
Then she passed, and she saw me : I ought not to
        care,
But I own I was hurt by her merciless stare.

Ah well, she "forgets" ; I had fancied she would ;
I hope she is happy—I 'm sure she is good ;
Come, Pet, it was she broke my heart, it is true ;
But I think you have mended it nicely : don't you?

EBB TIDE.

THINKING of thee, my lost one, far away,
  I watch the ebb tide creeping down the
    strand ;
The little boats come slowly in to land ;
The slanting sun announces close of day ;
The sails grow dusky, far out on the bay ;
  And still the placid sea, so near at hand,
  Creeps outward, murmuring across the sand,
And seeming life's great mystery to portray.

For life creeps slowly down the years, as here
  The sea recedes.   The pleasurers return,
    Happy and wearied, from their voyage at sea ;
And I, perchance, shall find my vision clear,
  When the last rays of my own sunset burn,
    And I shall go yet farther, dear, from thee.

NANTASKET BEACH,
  July, 1890.

O MA REINE !

FROM a heart that has learned what it is to be
    broken,
In the world's unrelenting and pitiless school,
With the thought that lies deepest remaining un-
    spoken,
I send you the greetings and blessings of Yule.
And oh ! if your own heart no longer discloses
    Regard for the sacred and beautiful past,
While mine wears its sackcloth and ashes of roses,
    I pray you remember I loved to the last.

CHRISTMAS, 1839.

I WILL BE PATIENT.

" PATIENT?" Have I not long been patient,
    dear,
Hoping against all hope, and holding fast
To one pure love that on my soul hath cast
A radiance star-like, lustrous, fixed and clear,
And made me face all ills, devoid of fear,
    Save for the fear of God? Have I not passed
    Through months of sorrow, hoping, at the last,
That through the clouds some sunshine might ap-
    pear?

I will be patient yet. But as the hart
    Pants for the waterbrooks, so yearns my soul;
Let me but know, while we must bide apart,
    You too are praying soon to reach the goal;
Dear, gentle woman! Sorrow hath no dart
    To strike a wound your love could not make
    whole.

IN ILLNESS.

IT MAY be this is but a passing ill,
  Or it may be the solemn final call
Which may come soon or late, but comes to all.
—I bow to the Almighty Father's will.
Through heart-aches, saddening all my days, I still
  Have kept my faith in him.   Death's somber pall
May shroud me round, but though its shadows fall
Across my life, my soul they cannot fill.

One word, one last regret, to that dear one
  Whom I have loved :   *The half she never knew.*
    God gave, he well may claim, my fitful breath ;
His mercy will not fail.   When life is done,
  Though this poor frame be prey to frost and dew,
    I shall have solved the mystery called Death.

THE MATCHLESS.

UNTO the sky, one star,
  Round which the myriads roll,
Clear shining from afar,
  True to the pole.

Unto the field, one flower,
  The fairest Nature knows,
Emblem of kingly power—
  The royal rose.

Unto the sea, one pearl,
  Hid in some cave unknown,
Where long sea-grasses curl
  About its throne.

Unto my soul, one love—
  God's light upon my brow,
Descending from above ;
  And that love—THOU.

TO SLEEP.

A FTER all the pleadings, all the prayers and
tears,
After humble penitence, and a hope to be
Nobler, better, braver, through the coming years,
What but vain repinings now are left to me?
Was my sin so grievous that I may not see
Any hope of finding from my grief release?
Come, O Sleep, and take me, take me back to
thee ;
Bear me back to Dreamland, where alone is peace.

MABEL'S HANDKERCHIEF.

HOW WILL death come to me? I sometimes
ask ;
And in what spot will be prepared my grave?
I may find rest beneath the ocean's wave,
Or it may be when busy at my task
That I shall see stern Death remove his mask ;
But I—I have no trembling fears to brave ;
Why should I care these bitter drops to save,
That flow so slowly from life's brittle flask?

But when some friendly hand shall seek my heart,
To see if it be still, there shall be found
The token of a love that could not die.
To speak her name my lips will no more part,
And nought will then avail to heal my wound ;
But she will know none worshiped her as I.

WAITING.

(A ROUNDEL.)

I SHALL be waiting, dear, in that glad day
  When you will come and say: "Love, I am
    here."
It may be soon, or years be passed away;—
  I shall be waiting, dear.

So that I keep your love, hope shineth clear;
  Loving and longing, learning how to pray,
I wait until the blest day shall draw near.

When I may turn to you once more, and say:
  "My Mabel," all our griefs shall disappear;
Ah, forget not,—let life bring what it may—
  I shall be waiting, dear.

BELOVËD.

"BELOVËD!" Let me write the old-time word,
Which once you prized, and called me to repeat;
Time has been cruel, but he cannot cheat
Our ears of all the loving vows they heard
When by a common thought our hearts were stirred;
    My lips can frame no word to be more sweet;
    And if I suffer failure and defeat,
Love still lives on, though hope be long deferred.

I do not know when we shall meet again,
    Nor what will be my welcome in that hour;
I know I love you now, dear, more than then,
    Just as the bud bursts open into flower;
And I shall speak the dear old word, and when
    You answer, oh, remember all your power!

POTOMAC RIVER,
February, 1891.

A VISION.

SHADOW from out the beautiful past,
Why do you come to me, in my gloom?
Your great sad eyes make my heart beat fast ;
You still are sweet as a rose in bloom ;
You still are tender and grave and kind,—
And how can you know an old wound's smart?—
How sadly comes the truth to my mind,
I have your presence : he has your heart.

Hopes and dreams of mine, good and pure,
Have lost the sunlight and felt the rain ;
Futures whose promises seemed so sure,
Were only castles builded in Spain.
Do you wonder, then, that, coming near,
My words should falter and quick tears start?
Or that I think, when meeting you, dear,
I have your presence : he has your heart?

Did Love deceive you, in the old days?
  Were you wrong to think you loved me then?
I wish I knew all Love's secret ways :
  I would try to set you wrong again.
No, not that, dear, if you love him more,
  Though my life loses its better part ;
I can pray : God bless you ! as before,
  But oh, I would that I had your heart !

PLYMOUTH CHIMES.

A T FIVE o'clock, each afternoon,
I go my homeward way,
And as I climb up Chestnut Hill,
From the great stone church, so dark and still,
The chimes begin to play;
And little matters it what tune.
They ring, now loud, now tenderly,
In sweet, melodious babel,
But all it seems to say to me
Is: *Mabel—Mabel—Mabel—*

I know she waits, intent to hear
My step within the gate;
She notes the hour: it 's almost time,
And as she hears the distant chime,
She wonders if I 'm late.
And every sound that strikes her ear

Makes her to give a little start,
  While all the time she 's humming
Some tune whose music to her heart
  Says : *Coming—coming—coming—*

I turn the corner, and at last
  Am at my own home door ;
She meets me, and within her eyes
Shines the fond welcome that I prize ;
  So Love is glad once more.
The toils, the worries, all are past ;
My heart leaps up, and on my cheek
  Her welcome kiss is proving
All that her lips could find to speak
  Of : *Loving—loving—loving—*

      .   .   .   .   .

How sweet ye rang, O Plymouth Chimes,
  On that day long ago !
Why did I weep to hear you play,
When up the hill I walked, today,
  So falteringly and slow ?
You bore me back to other times ;
And did you see the sad tears start,
  And hear her dear name spoken ?—
That all you murmured to my heart
  Was : *Broken—broken—broken—*

By walks where we were used to go,
 And even to the door,
I pass ; but she on other things
Is bent ; no smile my coming brings,
 As in the days before.
My footstep now she would not know ;
And ah ! far off I hear the bells,
 Whose theme seems now of mourning,
And of her feeling only tells
 Of : *Scorning—scorning—scorning—*

O bells, you jangle ! Cease your chime :
 The parting hour is near ;
My heart in ashes mourns today,
Since I forever go away
 From her, to me so dear.
Oh, whisper to her of that time
When we were happy, and since now
 My lips may not caress her,
Oh, tell her of my loving vow,
 And pray : *God bless her—bless her—*

THANKSGIVING DAY.

L ET others be thankful, and join in rejoicing;
  My own heart is sad, and my skies are grown
    gray;
My greeting is gay, but the words are not voicing
  The sadness that fills me this Thanksgiving Day.
Oh, what are the feasting, the rout and the pleasure?
  Though Fame has been kind to me, what can she
    do
To make me forget that I lost my one treasure?—
  Oh, what is Thanksgiving Day, dear, without you?

1890.

IF DREAMS WERE ONLY DREAMS.

EVEN in sleep your face still looks on me,
    O my belovëd ! and behold, last night
An old familiar place came to my sight,
And dear old friends, whose hearts of care were free,
Who said : "What ! still unchanged?   How can
        it be?
Look at her—never heart was half so light ;
She has forgotten you."
                    Ah, they were right ;
Dreams are realities, sometimes, you see.

So I awoke, and found my lashes wet,
    My eyes abrim with sorrowful great tears ;
        I marked my hand, within the moon's broad
            gleam,
Trembling with anguish, while my lips, firm set,
    Kept back the vain wish from unheeding ears :
        Oh, if my dream were nothing but a dream !

POPPIES.

SOFT wreaths of smoke float slowly into air ;
  My tear-stained eyelids close, heavy with
    sleep,
  Forgetting, for a little, how to weep ;
Drowsiness comes, an angel unaware,
Then visions of green fields and waters fair,
  And picture-clouds that through the azure sweep ;
  Sorrow is vanquished, and dreams soft and deep
Come to dispel my dark thoughts of despair.

Alas for waking ! Why must slumber cease ?
  Sleep, blesséd Sleep, be merciful and kind ;
Send me not back to grief that must increase :
  Burn out Woe's great sad eyes, and make him
      blind. . . .
My dear Love bade me go and seek for peace :
  And this is peace. How sad a peace to find !

PERIWINKLE.

FLOWERS of the Maytime,
  Blooming by the wall,
Stars of Summer's daytime,
  Twinkling at her call,
In the fragrant morning,
  Down the garden close,
I have sought you, scorning
  E'en the Jacqueminots.

Slender-stemmed, up-gazing
  From the glossy green,
Toward the blue up-raising
  Heads in royal mien,
You are welcome comers,
  Harbingers of June,
Whispering that Summer 's
  Sure to greet us soon.

Spring has brought you hither
   In her diadem ;
Sad that you must wither,
   Severed from the stem ;
Birds are making babel
   In the leafy shade ;
You should go to Mabel,
   If you would not fade.

Blossom in seclusion,
   In the garden old ;
Birds may make intrusion,
   And the robins scold.
When a boy, I learned you,
   And your pretty name ;
Though the gardener spurned you,
   I upheld your fame.

Still I find you smiling
   In your wonted place ;
Still my feet beguiling
   Here to rest a space ;
Like the stars, you twinkle,
   In the blooming-time ;
Pretty Periwinkle,
   Blossom in my rhyme.

A RHYME AND A BOOK FOR MABEL.

T HE sailor from far lands
Brings silks and jewels home ;
The soldier, from the strife,
Trophies of victories ;
Neither brings empty hands.
And shall I idly roam,
Finding no gift to please
One who makes glad my life ?—
From his brief flight awing,
What shall your poet bring?

What, but some tender verse,
Some draught from the deep cup
Where glistens Love's sweet wine ?
It need not be my own,
So that the song rehearse
The wishes welling up

In my heart, that have flown
  To cheer you, Sweetheart mine !
One thing the book can do—
Witness I thought of you.

GREAT HEAD, WINTHROP,
  9 *August*, *1891.*

AT THE CONCERT.

W E SAT and heard the Master play
   Sweetly upon his violin,
And knew the music, grave or gay,
   Came from a throbbing heart within ;
We heard a whiskered "Signor" sing ;
   We heard "Monsieur" thump on the keys,
And from the poor piano wring
   The most heart-rending harmonies.

Then came a creature dressed in pink,
   Wasp-waisted, with a voice in E.
The program said she sang, I think ;
   I know I heard : "*Do, mi, sol, mi.*"
I could not write a long critique,
   But I should say this seraph frail
Seemed to be playing hide-and-seek
   Along the diatonic scale.

But Mabel, at my left, spoke low
   (She understands that sort of thing) :
"She 's lovely ! don't you call her so?
   And don't you like to hear her sing?"
"My dear," I sighed, "she suits your taste?
   Well, as to music, I 'm a dunce,
But my thought was : I like a waist
   'Round which an arm will go but once !"

LOVE'S QUERY.

WHAT makes my heart go pit-a-pat,
    When Mabel's eyes look into mine?
Why do I find it hard to chat
And to cold words my thoughts confine?

Perhaps because her charms divine
    I may not hope to win.   Is that
    What makes my heart go pit-a-pat,
When Mabel's eyes look into mine?

Ah, is it aught to wonder at—
    That I should wish her love were mine?
Now that you know I dream of that,
    Can you not read the tell-tale sign?
What makes my heart go pit-a-pat,
    When Mabel's eyes look into mine?

WHEN MY SHIP COMES IN.

I, MABEL dearest, seek your hand
And heart, at Cupid's sweet command,
And fondly pray your eyes of blue
To smile upon me, when I woo
And whisper of "*la passion grande*."

How now?   "Have I," you ask, "the 'sand'
'Gainst Life's rude buffetings to stand
And guard you, ever brave and true?"
—Aye, Mabel dear !

"And may you drive your four-in-hand?
And spend the 'season' at the strand?
And on 'old masters' feast your view?"
Aye ! all will I bestow on you,
All—when, of course you understand,
I 'm able, dear !

1886.

A VALENTINE TO MY LOVE AT VASSAR.

SAINT VALENTINE, 't was this thy day
On which, of old, the legends say,
The birds were wont to mate and woo ;
And we have kept the custom, too.

My love and I are leagues apart,
Yet well she knows she has my heart ;
And she has promised to be mine—
My well-belovëd Valentine.

I see her, sitting all alone.—
In growing wise, how fair she 's grown !—
One hand supports her damask cheek :
She 's poring o'er tomorrow's Greek.

Ah me, if I might sit, tonight,
There in her study, warm and bright,
And, throwing off my cares the while,
Bask in the sunshine of her smile !

Alas, no sweet face lights the gloom
Here in my cheerless, lonely room ;
But I am faithful at her shrine,
And send to her a valentine.

I see her take it in her hands ;
She bursts the wrappings and the bands ;
And then her cheek begins to glow,
And little dimples come and go.

My Valentine, I chose thee well ;
What else could thus her smiles compel?
She calls her friends ; straightway appears
A flock of lovely, envious dears.

A chorus of delighted "Oh !'s"
Bursts forth, and well my lady knows
That she is queen since this has come—
My ten-pound box of choice new gum !

BALLADE OF A PLEASANT RECOLLECTION.

WHEN moved by some fair maid's decree,
    Who could refuse a rhyme to write?
Not I, for one ! and when the plea
    Is made by one whose eyes are bright
    As yours, the wish I dare not slight ;
But as for themes, I find none handy.
    Yet stay ! do you recall that night
When we gay friends made " 'lasses " candy ?

Do you remember it, *m'amie?*—
    How Bert and I the nuts did smite ?
And how I held upon my knee
    Something I thought—not—very—light?—
    The jesting words that we, despite
Our dignity, found time to bandy?—
    Ah me, how swift the hours took flight,
When we gay friends made " 'lasses " candy !

I wonder if this memory
    Which brings to me such keen delight,
Will, in your heart and Mabel's, be
    Remembered as perhaps it might
    If it had been some fairer knight—
Not one with locks as rough and "sandy"
    As mine, you 'd chosen to invite,
When we gay friends made "'lasses" candy.

Envoy.

Maude, to find favor in your sight
    Your poet prays : at your command, he
Has made this rhyme about that night
    When we gay friends made "'lasses" candy.

OFF THE STAGE.

PROUDLY I take her down the hall;
    I know she draws the glance of all,
        And it is rated
A boon to win her smile's cold charm.
Blanche rests on mine her snowy arm,—
        And I 'm elated !

Beth paints me pretty little things;
She thrums for me her banjo's strings,—
        And not so badly;
She 's bright, and when she bids me : "Come
And see me—Thursdays I 'm at home,"
        I go most gladly.

And Maude?   At church, it 's very true,
I 've helped to fill the Van Dorn pew
        Many a Sunday;

They ask me in ; and they 've a sight
Of wealth, you see,—that sets me right
        With Mrs. Grundy.

But when beneath a midnight moon
I ride, who hears with me the tune
        Of the sweet sleighbells?
Blanche? Beth? Not they ! And Maude? Not hers
The hand I press, beneath the furs,
        For *that* is *Mabel's!*

1888.

THE MINSTREL AFIELD.

Harps are in every land
That await a voice that sings,
And a master-hand,—but the humblest hand
May gently touch the strings.

FATHER RYAN: Sentinel Songs.

CHRIST'S CHURCH.

WHAT matters it, my neighbor,
 That we be not agreed?
The Master counts the labor
 And love, more than the creed.
And if, God's word obeying,
 Each one his own way choose,
He still will hear us praying,
 Whatever form we use.

Though we may sing his praises
 In the Te Deum's strains,
The hymn our brother raises
 As kind a hearing gains ;
And under lofty arches,
 Or on the naked sod,
'T is one procession marches
 Up to the throne of God.

For you may find the leaven
  Where I should never search,
Without my guide to Heaven—
  Our Holy Mother Church.
Men, drawing from each other,
  Their temples build apart;
What profits it, my brother?
  Christ's church is in the heart.

ALL SAINTS, 1890.

JOHN BOYLE O'REILLY.

(DIED 10 AUGUST, 1890.)

WHILE the calm sea crept up and whispered
　　　to him,—
Ere broke the day,—
Without a word to those who loved and knew him,—
He passed away.

Just as his life its noblest height seemed crowning,
　　　In manhood's prime,
Gone all the trials, banished Fortune's frowning,
　　　God said : "'T is time."

Oh, how shall we, then, seek to understand it?
　　　It seems so strange ;
His work was waiting, ready, as he planned it,
　　　And then this change.

On that last night I slept almost beside him,
　　　And at the dawn
I found that Death had come, from earth to guide
　　　him,
　　　And he was gone.

Gone ! gone ! O sobs we know not how to smother,
        O tears that flow,
We loved him ! Poet, friend and tender brother,—
        Why should he go?

How sweet the music that had never failed him,
        How rich his store !
How fittingly and fondly had we hailed him :
        Our own Tom Moore !

O soul of love, O knightly heart and loyal,
        Death is not thine ;
Forever with the noble and the royal
        Thy name will shine.

In the great city to which dear ties bound him,
        But yesterday,
With the grand hosts of Freedom marching 'round
        him,
        Silent he lay.

He too had thought to see that mighty number
        Of warriors grim ;
He did not know that only peaceful slumber
        Was meant for him.

O Freedom, as thy heroes, in their splendor,
    March by thee, here,
Think of thy son, so loving, loyal, tender,—
    Spare him a tear.

We find some cheer our heavy grief to leaven,
    Some joy to win ;
We know that at the great white gate of Heaven
    He enters in.

He needs no tolling bell in any steeple,
    No requiem mass ;
From out the great affection of the people
    He may not pass.

We bring our tears : what more, now, can we proffer ?
    Behind his hearse
Humbly I walk, with all I have to offer—
    This love-born verse.

Thank God, we know, while grief our hearts is
        wringing,
    And all seems wrong,
Our sweet musician even now is singing
    A grand new song.

BEAU BRUMMELL.

TO RICHARD MANSFIELD.

WELL pictured, Mansfield !   Yours is earned
     applause ;
Your voice and look have quickened the dead
     past ;
And apt indeed this glance on History cast.
Brummell is dead, but Nature, to her laws
Faithful as ever, still repeats, and draws
   Such likenesses of men.   Ah, Time flies fast :
   Poor Beau !—a playwright's dummy at the last,—
The Prince of Fashion stripped of all his gauze.

Yet it is not all satire ; honest tears,
   At such a portraiture as this, must start.—
A man's life may be tinsel, but he hears,
   Sometimes, the soul's voice, and forgets his art ;
Kisses may live on lips long used to sneers ;
   And sometimes 'neath lace ruffles hides a heart.

WASHINGTON,
   10 February, 1891.

SENATOR HOAR.

JUST as Charles Sumner stood, within these walls,
 A living protest in the face of wrong,
That grand, calm figure in the turbulent throng,—
So, here, the voice of his apt pupil falls
In words befitting these historic halls ;
 And like a David, with his stone and thong,
 I see him turn his face, so fine, so strong,
Ever to front the foe, when duty calls.

Treason may hiss, and hate must have its sneer,
 But in the nation's grand historic tome
Our children's children, in some distant year,
 Will read of him, and make their hearts his home,
While Freedom sends his name, to her grown dear,
 Echoing forever 'round her matchless dome.

In the Senate Chamber at Washington,
 January, 1891.

FATHER McGLYNN.

(AFTER A MEETING WITH HIM, 13 MAY, 1889.)

I HEARD the gentle voice, whose speech
   Was simple, earnest, like the man,
And thought how far beyond his reach
   Lay the attainment of his plan ;
Yet, as his cordial hand clasped mine,
   In the swift kindling of his eye
I seemed to see his purpose shine—
   A purpose noble, pure and high.

Ah, let us who have doubted see
   Our own good deeds recalled, and then
Ask if we ever gave what he
   Has given for his fellow-men.
Laurels made ready for his head—
   Friends—fortune—power strong and sure—
"If these I must renounce," he said,
   "I do it gladly, for God's poor."

O noble-minded, pure-souled priest,
    Would there were more hearts like thine own ;
God will not count such with the least,
    When we are met about His throne.
Thy self-appointed work well done,
    Scorn never can its luster dim.
What though the Church disclaim her son ?
    Freedom an altar hath for him !

THE PROUDEST NAME.

TO MARY HOWE.

O SWEET young songstress of the North,
 Thy native hills have heard
No song so pure, so sweet, burst forth
 From any native bird.
It breathes the music of the rills
 That in thy mountains purl,
To welcome to her native hills
 A sweet New England girl.

Far over sea they spoke her praise
 In a strange foreign tongue ;
She came and charmed us with her ways,
 And loud our plaudits rung ;
Yet still she kept, with all her fame,
 That set two lands awhirl,
The simple manner that became
 A sweet New England girl.

She leaves again her native shore ;
  Be calm, ye seas that foam !
And when she comes, our hearts once more
  Will bid her welcome home.
And if she win, across the sea,
  The praise of lord and earl,
Let her remember still to be
  A sweet New England girl.

What stranger ever came and stirred
  Our hearts as she has done ?
What Old World singer ever heard
  Such plaudits as she won ?
Europe may search through cot and hall,
  And bring her rarest pearl,
But she is what is more than all—
  A sweet New England girl.

1888.

GROWING.

FOUR blithe summers, and four years' snows
Have passed her by. How the little maid
grows !—
Grows in winsomeness. grows more wise,—
Looks more roguishly out of those eyes,—
Finds such wonderful things each day,—
Gets so happily tired at play,—
Has her tears, till the clouds are past.—
Ah, but the little maid 's growing fast !

What does she think? Oh, she wonders why
The stars that twinkle are hung so high ;
What makes a little girl smile in the glass ;
Why so seldom the elephants pass ;
Why her kitten should chase its tail :
Why the boat has a big white sail ;—
These, and things we 've never found out,
Are what the little maid 's thinking about.

Margaret! Margaret! keep that smile;
You 'll be old in a little while;
Keep that laughter, and that sweet air;
Keep that little heart free from care;
Some day you 'll be tired of the toys;
Some day you 'll seek for grown-up joys;
Then you 'll have no treasures like these;
Keep them forever, so God please.

Down she goes, in the little white bed;
Love shall watch at the foot and the head;
When she comes back from Dreamland far,
She 'll be bright as the morning-star.
I shall pray, when she 's older yet,
Childhood's friends she may not forget.
Margaret, we 'll let the *years* go by:
Think, you 're a whole *day* older than I!

1891.

MY DEAD FRIEND.

(F. S. M., OBIIT 31 MARCH, 1888.)

THE clouds that veiled the sky in shadows dim
    Are gone at last ;
Into the peace withheld so long from him,
    His soul has passed.

It was not willed that he should find on earth
    Much happiness ;
His time of strength was small ; his meed of mirth
    Was even less.

Tasks light for others were to him not so ;
    He lacked the strength
To do his will : the books he longed to know
    Were closed at length.

The weary brain that study vexed too long
    Had done its best ;
The shattered frame that never had been strong
    Pleaded for rest.

The hearty sports that brought the flush of health
    To other boys,
He never knew; Death, drawing near by stealth,
    Took all his joys.

One solace only had he in his gloom—
    His violin ;
And as he played, alone, in the dark room,
    The light broke in.

He was not one to murmur : to his pain
    He seemed resigned ;
Forever kind, while life was on the wane,
    He grew more kind.

Stilled is the heart that was so generous,—
    Its suffering o'er ;
The lips that spoke but gentle words to us
    Will move no more.

Silent his well-loved violin : the strings
    Henceforth are dumb ;
Idle his bow,—no more to it he clings ;
    His call has come.

Tears blind our eyes ; we miss him from the path
    He with us trod ;
And yet, we know that joy at last he hath,—
    He is with God.

A PLEASANT RECEPTION.

I STAND before the open grate,
    And wonder much, the while I wait,
    She doesn't come and greet me ;
She knew I was to come today,
And why, then, should she be away,
    Instead of here to meet me ?

We are disposed, mayhap, to take
For granted that our friends should make
    Our own desires their pleasure ;
But still, she 's always, heretofore,
Been here to meet me at the door.
    Where is she now—the treasure ?

Ah, she is coming down the stairs ;
Perhaps I 'll catch her unawares ;
    But no : she comes—she sees me !

O golden hair ! O sweet blue eyes !
How much do I your owner prize,
    Although she does so tease me !

She laughs a merry laugh, and then
(Am I not favored man of men?)
    She kisses me *so* sweetly.
Her arms go 'round my neck, and she
Tells why she was so late : her plea
    Explains it most completely.

She takes my coat and gloves and hat ;
She sits me down, begins to chat,
    And—asks me what I 've brought her !
What 's that? "Who is it dares act so ?
My fiancée?" you ask? Oh no,—
    My darling little daughter !

1887.

THANKSGIVING.

WELCOME again, Thanksgiving,
    With winds however cold !
The spirit still is living
    That stirred our sires of old ;
And ever we remember
    Your blessing and your cheer,
For you have made November
    To all New England dear.

Let Winter fiercely brandish
    His weapons as he will ;
True sons of old Miles Standish,
    We meet him bravely still ;
And though his glove he flings us,
    In challenge for the fray,
God bless him, since he brings us
    Our own Thanksgiving Day.

What heart can find inviting
    Anger or enmity?
Today we are uniting
    Around the family tree.
Let Hatred go and bury
    His harsh and evil creed,
And we will make a merry
    Thanksgiving Day indeed.

And let the poor be sharers
    In all our festal mirth,
That we may be the bearers
    Of Christ's goodwill on earth;
Set the good cheer aflowing,
    And Gloom may hide away,
Since every heart is knowing
    This is Thanksgiving Day.

1890.

THE MARCH OF THE HEROES.

TO MY FATHER.

OFF with your hats, young men ;
    Heroes are passing by !
No trappings of grim war
They bear, as once they bore,
But through these streets again
They march, as once before
They marched, when going forth,—
The flower of the North,—
To conquer or to die.

Flowers are in their hands,
Where once was steel, instead.
To meet no fiery foe,
Through the calm streets they go ;
They hear no stern commands,
But music sad and slow ;
Not for the living, they
March by us, here, today,
But for the noble dead.

Not stalwart as of old,
But bent with swift-sped years ;
Grizzled of beard and hair,
I see them passing there.
Sons of such sires, behold !
Those wavering ranks declare
Whence comes your manliness.
May Heaven the living bless :
To the dead, grateful tears.

O sire of mine, well done !
Thou marchest in that line,
Old comrades at thy side.
When thy wronged country cried,
Thou wast her worthy son.
My heart leaps up in pride ;
Down through long years to be,
Posterity shall see
Thy deed in glory shine.

Under the skies of May,
They move where lie the lost ;
Garlands for every grave ;
Over the silent brave
Flowers shall smile today,
And feathery grasses wave.
Their glory cannot wane

Who purchased peace through pain,
Though love and life it cost.

Bloom for them, roses rare.
Unfurl, O flag of light,
Unto the gentle breeze ;
Over brave hearts like these
Thou shinest doubly fair.
To guard our liberties,
God make us worthy sons
Of these enhaloed ones—
Soldiers of truth and right !

30 MAY, 1891.

THAT DEAREST OF DAYS.

WE loitered along by the shore of the lake ;
  We watched the birds on the wing ;
And the drowsy day seemed but half awake,
  So quiet was everything.
We heard, at times, the plash of an oar
  From some lazily-moving boat,
And over the lake, near the Shrewsbury shore,
  Saw a fish-hawk hover and float ;
And all, in the haze of the afternoon,
  And the smile of the summer skies,
Seemed lulled into dreams as by some sweet tune
  As tender, my dear, as your eyes.

The soft breeze rustled the leaves overhead ;
  The chipmunks chattered at will ;
A dry twig snapped 'neath a rabbit's tread :
  All else in the woods was still.

We had no need, in the silence, for speech—
    Mere words would have sounded rough ;
But our eyes told all in the heart of each,
    And that was more than enough.
I pressed in my hand your finger-tips,
    And your cheeks—what made them to flame?
The only language that moved my lips
    Was a murmuring of your name.

Whenever I think of that dearest of days,
    My heart of a sudden grows weak,
And the longing light in my eyes betrays
    What the blush betrayed on your cheek.
The clouds may darken the skies, and the lake
    Lose the beauty it had that day ;
The birds their way to the south may take,
    And the woods grow cheerless and gray ;
But the light of your eyes, and the tender words
    That we spoke, are lingering yet ;
And though the summer may go with the birds,
    That day we can never forget.

AFTERWARD.

WHEN, with some other arm in yours, you go
Down through the streets we trod that
happy night,
Will you recall, with thought however light,
The one who, by your side, with heart aglow,
And voice that faltered or at times spoke low,
Walked on, enraptured with a new delight,
Scarce knowing if he dreamed, or heard aright,
And fondly wished it might be ever so?

And when, light-hearted still, you pass that way,
Will you remember that I walk alone,
Finding no voice to answer mine and say
All the dear speeches that your lips have known,
And growing sad, because, from day to day,
I miss the impulse of that look and tone!

GHOSTS.

INTO a night of dreams and broken rest
   Come all the evil ghosts of years gone by,
To look upon me with reproachful eye,
And tell of deeds wherein I have transgressed.

Dark secrets hidden long within my breast
   They seem to shout to all the earth and sky,
   And uttering, in my sleep, a frightened cry,
I wake to find my heart with fear oppressed.

When wakening comes, fond lips still turn to press
   Their kisses on my cheek, grown white and thin,
Dear arms still clasp me in a fond caress,
   And love is still as it hath ever been ;
Yet one stain mars its every tenderness—
   The ghastly phantom of an old-time sin !

THE VENTURE-BARK OF HOPE.

FURL all her tattered sails, and from the peak
    Take her starred pennant down ;
No more the distant seas her keel shall seek ;
No more the storm on her its anger wreak ;
    No more to favoring winds her canvas spread ;
      Let her smooth sides grow brown :   .
    My hope in her is dead.

Her single venture has been sailed.   In vain
      She sought the far-off land
Where she might find what I had hoped to gain —
The magic gem that for my weary pain
    A gentle balm and sweet relief should bring.
      She lies by yonder strand,
    And hope has taken wing.

Oh, that she might have foundered far away,
      Rather than thus return !
Better to sunken shoal or reef a prey
Than thus in idle quiet to decay.

Then might my heart at least have dared to hope ;
    Now it can only yearn
For light, and, blinded, grope.

O wreckéd bark ! I ventured all in thee ;
    And now, with tattered sail,
And scarred from battling with the angry sea,
Thou reachest port and answereth to me :
    "Thy dream hath been in vain—an idle quest."
    Oh, that it thus should fail ! . . .
Can it be for the best ?

   .   .   .   .   .

My heart hath hidden from all other eyes
    Its silent, bitter grief :
Dear Father, thou alone hast heard its cries,
And when, grown weary of its fate, it dies,
    Thou only canst know all that it hath borne,—
    Thou only bring relief,
And bid it cease to mourn.

No solace can the present to me bring.
    . One sad, one fond mistake
Has blighted hope and love and everything ;
I have no longer aught by which to cling ;
    So my heart suffers, in its anguish keen,
    Until it one day break ;
And then—the Great Unseen !

PINE GROVE SCHOOL.

FOR M. S. B.

THE murmuring pines have watched for years
   The comings-in and goings-out,
And heard, no doubt, as Nature hears,
   The class-room hum or play-time shout.

Their branches, bending with the snow,
   Have darkened winter afternoons,
Or, swayed by breezes to and fro,
   Have lent their fragrance to the Junes.

And through this doorway childish feet
   Have dragged, at many a morning-time,
When Nature's music seemed most sweet,
   And Wisdom's heights most hard to climb.

O children of the wayside school !
   You linger here, in shade and sun,
Not much perplexed by task or rule ;
   Yet here are battles to be won.

On you the state has set her eyes—
  The mother-eyes of love and pride ;
She waits ; she whispers : "They will rise,
  And take their station by my side ;

"The sober minds, the willing hearts,
  Lovers of God and Truth and Right,
Masters of all the honest arts,—
  In them behold my noblest might."

Go on, then, as the way be shown,
  And weather Life's tempestuous gales,
And each an honest name make known
  Through all these sweet Lancastrian vales.

And she who points to you the way—
  Her work its meed of honor brings ;
Listen : you hear our mother say :
  "My children do no greater things."

Not to her sages does she look
  To make her foremost of the earth ;
She gives you slate and spelling-book,
  And says : "Be worthy of your birth."

Dear Massachusetts !   Let her fill
  A thousand books with laws and rules ;
Here is her wisest statecraft still :
  God bless her for her common schools !

LANCASTER, *June, 1890.*

GRANDMAMMA.

TIME long since cracked her feeble voice ;
    Her eyes are now grown dim ;
Yet, finding reason to rejoice,
    She quavers through the hymn.
She cannot keep the time or key,
    But all her slips are drowned,
Unnoticed, save perhaps by me,
    In the great organ's sound.

Once her young voice rang clear and sweet
    In the old-fashioned choir,
And made at least one brave heart beat
    With quickening desire ;
Still joining in the swell of song,
    Telling to God her praise,
She scarcely thinks her voice less strong
    Than in her girlhood days.

Poor broken voice ! Yet why the thought?
    Soon it will be made whole ;
E'en now may not God's ear have caught
    The music of that soul?
And when, ere long, she lifts her voice
    In the great choir sublime,
Her praise will sound where all rejoice,
    And none sing out of time.

IN OLD SAINT JOHN'S.

SWEET boyish voices in the choir,
    Ye fall upon my ears
In strains that unto praise inspire,
    Or melt my heart to tears.
Through painted windows streams the sun ;
    The white-robed priests intone ;
And as my soul's prayer is begun,
    I make your plea my own.

And in this sweetly solemn place,
    Where falls the sunlight dim,
I see the blessed Master's face,
    And turn my eyes on Him.
O heart of mine, once pure, but long
    To ways of sin enticed,
Come, let us kneel, with prayerful song,
    Here at the feet of Christ.

Blest consolation !   Let me make
  Confession of my sin,
And, by the faith I cherish, take
  Christ's word my heart within ;
For me He died, for me He lives,
  In the Most Holy Three,
And perfect absolution gives,
  My soul from sin to free.

Shall I not cheerfully resign
  A world so filled with strife,
When He, my gracious Lord divine,
  For me gave up His life !
Let me be filled with power of grace,
  And sacred fervor deep,
So may my heart, in every place,
  Its Lent forever keep.

Washington,
  February, 1891.

AT VESPERS.

"LET us confess our sins." I hear the priest
    As one who listens in a waking dream;
My soul looks up to God; and lo! I seem
To see a table spread as for a feast.
The Prodigal's return! My shame hath ceased;
A waiting Father's glad eyes on me beam.
So much hath he forgiv'n! nor will he deem
His wayward son deserving love the least.

"According to thy promises." Blest word!
    My soul looks upward, turning unto him;
    My penitence God knoweth; I abide
Within his promise. He my prayer hath heard.
    In answering token there, in vision dim,
    I see the Cross and my Lord crucified.

A MOHAMMEDAN.

"God is but one God."
THE KORAN.

IN the rose attar land, the boy first heard
   The chimes that call the Faithful unto prayer;
   He knelt in reverence on the mosque's broad stair,
And as the young soul, like a timid bird,
Sought and yet feared to fly, his heart was stirred
   By the first precept he saw written there :
   "God is but one God," from the Korân, where
The True Believer reads the Master's word.

Shall I come less near Christ, if I, too, say :
   "God is but one God" ?   Shall my brother fear
   That he is not to reach the longed-for goal?
Nay ; let us kneel together when we pray ;
   I know that prayer to Allah God will hear,
   Because I know the whiteness of that soul.

UNPREPARED.

WHEN I was ill, there came to me one night
 A sad-browed angel, wrapped in gloom, who laid
His hand on mine, and said : "Be not afraid ;
'Tis thy friend, Death : art ready for thy flight?"
And in my heart there was no trace of fright,
 So, answering him, I smiled, and calmly said :
 "I am prepared,—my peace with God is made ;
I do not fear to stand before his light."

"Thy peace with God?" The angel shook his head :
 "Bethink thee, then, of thy poor brother man ;
 Are there no erring ones still unredeemed?
Are there no homeless orphans still unfed?
 Hast thou no chance to be Samaritan?"
 And lo, he passed away, and I had dreamed !

1889.

MY MORNING WALK HOME.

(AFTER THE PAPER GOES TO PRESS.)

TIRED out, after my long night's work,
And glad to start for home,
I make friends with the shades that lurk
In the dim morning gloom;
And in my solitary walk
I do not lack for cheer;
Nature herself is there to talk,
And never tires my ear.

I drink deep draughts of the fresh air
Cool with the morning dew;
The world seems stilled as if in prayer,
And I feel reverent, too.
The city sleeps; there are no sounds,
Save for the steady feet
Of the patrolman on his rounds
Along the quiet street.

But as I plod my way along,
 My heart finds voice to sing,
And, softly, some familiar song
 Upon the air I fling ;
And then, as if 't were only still
 Until the first should break
The sleepy silence and the chill,
 Old Earth begins to wake.

Far in the east a rosy light
 Begins to tinge the sky,
Telling that Sol, in splendor dight,
 Will greet us by and by.
A southwind, warm and soft and thin,
 Comes rustling through the trees,
And all the birdikins begin
 To pipe their morning glees.

The stars have long since flickered out ;
 Aurora's blush grows deep ;
And early risers stir about,
 Still drowsy from their sleep ;
The milkmen, with their noisy carts,
 Begin to rattle by ;
A little newsboy by me darts,
 His ragged cap awry.

By houses where my luckier friends
  Still lie in Slumber's arms,
I plod my way, until it ends,
  With all its morning charms.
And while the world roars through the day,
  In dreams my cares take flight;
Sleep, blessed Sleep, comes to repay
  The toilers of the night.

SKELETONS.

SINCE sheep first grazed, the old saws say,
  Each flock has had one lambkin sable,
And men who hate to see folk gay
  Declare one sits at every table.
"Beneath the smile the heart is cold."
  "' Tis fear that gives us proper meekness."
Alas ! if all the truth be told,
  These stabs lay bare our dearest weakness.

If we 've no sheep whose antics bring
  Disgrace upon our present station,
We know he lived and had his fling
  In the preceding generation.
Grim skeletons we all possess !
  Dark guests who never leave their lodgings !
Worse than the duns who round us press,
  With them avail not all our dodgings.

There 's Jones—grown rich, from toil set free,
And longing to indulge ambition;
He 'd like to write : "John Jones, *M. C.*,"
But could he reach that proud position?
He fears to run, lest his campaign
Should plunge his good name in disaster,
Because he wears the Grim Past's chain,
And Secret is his hardest master.

Who knows his neighbor?   You and I
Have had our times of curious wonder:
What makes me shun the Long-Gone-By?
What Ghost is yours to tremble under?
Dark is the mystery of each;
You 've had some folly, but—what was it?
You know my specter lurks in reach,—
Yet you have never seen the closet.

When no one else is near at hand,
We like to take our ghosts from hiding.
Grim, grinning ghouls ! they understand
What we are never heard confiding.
We know how long the past endures,
We know what secrets men must smother;
For I have mine, and you have yours,
And neither one deceives the other !

A MESSAGE.

(A RONDEL FOR A FAN.)

G O, pretty fan, and bear from me
    Kind wishes to my lady fair,—
  Dear friendship, kindly thought and care,
And hope that she may happy be.

Wish her untold prosperity,
  And joy and health beyond compare ;
  Go, pretty fan, and bear from me
Kind wishes to my lady fair.

My kindest thoughts are hers, as she,
  Without this rhyme, is well aware ;
  But since I know not when or where
We meet again, I say to thee :
Go, pretty fan, and bear from me
  Kind wishes to my lady fair.

THE CANNON SHOT AT FORTRESS MONROE.

IN peaceful pyramids at rest they lie,
　　Grim, dark reminders of war passed away ;
　　Blue are the skies above the smiling bay,
And off toward Newport News one may descry
The white-winged merchantmen go sailing by,
　　Where once the Congress and her consort lay,
　　And where the Monitor, that famous day,
Made all the world look on with wondering eye.

Still the old fortress keeps its warlike air,
　　But its great guns are silent, and these balls
May lie unmoved, and rust and crumble there ;
　　Only the bugle-note or drum-beat falls
Upon the breeze, for Peace is everywhere,
　　And War is History's dream that she recalls.

1891.

COMEDY.

The conjurer comes with his rings
And his Punch and Judy show.

AUSTIN DOBSON: The Street Singer.

Our hearts are young 'neath wrinkled rind—
Life 's more amusing than we thought.

ANDREW LANG: Ballade of Middle Age.

THE UNEXPECTED.

SHE was the reigning belle !
　　Straightway in love I fell ;
Potent became the spell,—
　　Too plain for masking.
Then for a time I wooed,
For her sweet favor sued,
Till I 'd my courage screwed
　　Up to the "asking."

Out of the glare and heat,
Where to the music's beat
Tripped the untiring feet
　　Of the gay dancer,
Gently I led my fair
Partner, so debonair,
Told her the whole, and there
　　Waited her answer.

Sweet was the flowers' perfume,
Weird the enshadowing gloom;
From the gay, lighted room
    Sweet strains came faintly;
Turning, she smiled, and blushed,
Murmured surprise, and flushed,
Then, in the silence hushed,
    Answered me quaintly.

Doubtless you think she said,
When she had raised her head,
That which all lovers dread:
    "She 'd be my sister."
That 's where you 've made a guess
Wrong, as you must confess;
For she said softly: "Yes !"
    Yes ! and I kissed her !

A FAIR GAMBLER.

GRACE, though a belle, and gay,
Has notions that today
Most of the girls scarce pay
    A moment's thought to ;
Politics she thinks "grand !"
She knows she 'd understand
The ruling of the land ;—
    I 'm sure she ought to !

We wagered, for we run
To different faiths. Great fun !
She bet on Harrison,
    And I on Grover :
A dozen kisses she
Owed if it went to me.
(Oh, how I prayed G. C.
    Might still "hold over.")

If she won, I must buy
Twelve pounds of Huyler's.   I
Cannot, of course, deny
   I hoped she 'd lose it.
So Tuesday came, and Fate
Left me disconsolate,
My ill luck to berate,
   And loudly abuse it.

Today was the time set ;
I went to pay my bet,
And on the steps I met
   Her handsome cousin.
We bowed ; he smiled, I thought,
To see what I had brought ;
Then I went in, but not
   To get that DOZEN !

What had so moved Miss Grace ?
Blushes suffused her face ;
She smoothed a rumpled lace :
   A vague impression—
That cousin !—swept over me ;
But, turning suddenly
(Her conscience pricked, you see),
   She made confession :

"You see, a week ago
I feared I'd lose, and so
I—'hedged,' you call it?—Oh,
  How good ! you 've brought them."
Alas, the artful maid !
I for her bonbons paid ;
The kisses that I prayed—
  That cousin got them !

1888.

IN QUARANTINE.

ONE short week since I had not thought
That I could ever be by aught
    So sore afflicted ;
I pass the house within whose walls
She is, and may not stop : my calls
    Are interdicted.

Alas, how fitful is our bliss !
I may not go to her, and this
    By her own order.
Here is the note she wrote it in,—
To me !—to me, who long have been
    Her heart's sole warder.

The grand stone steps I mount no more ;
I may not enter, as before,
    And clasp her to me ;

Save for a dim light in her room,
The house is silent, wrapped in gloom ;—
    I too am gloomy !

Not that she loves me less, although
I 'm exiled to my studio
    And long-shunned easels ;
But her small brother (poor dear lad !)
Has got—what I have never had,
    Hang it !—the measles !

MY NEIGHBOR SWEET.

A FESTIVAL MEMORY.

HER seat is just across the aisle ;
  Coming, we always meet, or going ;
And oh ! she is so free from guile—
  Sweet as a rosebud freshly blowing !

You will not wonder that my mind
  Sometimes plays truant to the singing,
For wheresoe'er the heart 's inclined,
  The thoughts are sure to go a-winging.

She wears a smile : I hardly think
  That I could tell what else she 's wearing ;
It might be blue—perhaps it 's pink ;
  I 'll not seem rude to her through staring.

And all the "nicest" boys she knows ;
  They crowd about at intermission ;
I do not think she means to "pose"—
  I 'll harbor no such supposition.

Never a concert misses she,
  Be it in afternoon or even,
And so the glory seems to be
  A little more like that of Heaven.

Dear little saint! she likes to go ;
  Sad thought—though fortune so allows her,
Save for the books, she would not know
  "The Golden Legend" from "Tannhäuser !"

1890.

TEMP–RA MUT–NT–R.

A T college we had stood together,
    The closest sort of chums,
Till Alma Mater loosed our tether,
    With deep encomiums;
Later, I chanced to be left over
    An hour in Gotham town,
Thought of the days we 'd spent in clover,
    And went to find Ned Brown.

Cabby stopped where the "d'rect'ry" stated;
    The name was on the door;
Inside, I sat a time and waited
    My dear old friend of yore.
Ned's sister came to entertain me,
    Of course—her brother's chum.
Why, Gotham town, shouldst thou constrain me
    Into such snares to come?

We talked of music, art, "the season,"
The last Assembly ball.
Could I wish Ned more prompt, with reason?
Ah, really, not at all.
But when he came, what hearty greeting !
No more could be desired ;
I was so glad of such a meeting,—
So sorry *she* retired !

Gotham, since then I 've learned to know you,
And all your thoroughfares.
Stop ! *No. 10.* I need n't show you
What name the doorplate bears ;
Once it had never met my vision,
When first I rang the bell ;
Now that I walk in fields Elysian,
I know it fairly well.

Inside, I find the same surroundings ;
They 've now a friendly air ;
The poor piano knows my poundings ;
I have my special chair ;
And Ned, with gloves and hat, chats, standing
Ready to go down town,
And leaves, on hearing, from the landing,
The rustle of a gown !

THE NEW RILEY.

THE fad among the poets now is imitating Jim;
    They make their verses tumble down in
        sections, just like him;
The Whitcomb Riley ending leads you down to an
        abyss;
                                    This.
                        Like
            Up
Suppose we change the thing and boost 'em

Suppose you are describing how you met a summer
        girl,
And wooed, and won, and lost her, in Narragan-
        sett's whirl;
You thought you had your heiress hooked and
        landed high and dry,
                                    High.
                        Sky
            Knocked
But she was fooling and your plans got

Perhaps you 're on the street, and make your plans
    to be a bear ;
You buy a lot of wheat " dirt cheap," and then you
    get a scare ;
You let it go for nothing, and before quotations
    close,
                      Goes.
               She
       Up
It takes a sudden spurt, you see, and

And scores of things might be described with like
    poetic wiles,
The theater hat, the iceman's bill—all Eiffel tower
    styles ;
With novelties and mark-down sales, and bargain
    lots in rhyme,
                    Climb.
             To
       Got
If you expect to sell your wares, you 've

Then here 's to Jimmy Riley, the feller wot kin
    spell
In the style of old Josh Billings, although not quite
    so well ;

We 've learned that if a poet can make his thinker
   hop,
                                        Top.
                               On
                    Keep
And write a ladder-poem, he can

1890.

AT THE END OF THE WALTZ.

GO now, Dear Fan ; she will not see
The kiss I 've hidden in your fringes ;
I may not dream that thoughts of me
 Will cause the blush her cheek that tinges.

But when you softly meet her lips,
 My fond caress shall leave its hiding,
And, mingling in that sweet eclipse,
 Render my boldness past her chiding.

NOTES.

NOTES.

TO THEE, BELOVED.

These lines were sent from Washington, Christmas, 1890, with roses and a copy of Louise Chandler Moulton's "In the Garden of Dreams."

LOVE SAW THE LIKENESS.

Going through the Corcoran Gallery of Art, one day in Christmas week of 1890, I came suddenly upon a portrait, unnumbered and untitled, which bore a strong resemblance to One far away, though on close scrutiny the fine lines of the face seemed stern, rather than gentle, as in the face of the One I knew. I sought out the owner of the picture, who had brought it from Paris. It is a new conception of Charlotte Corday, usually represented as in prison, but here in a street habit, outside the door of the bath where she slew Marat. Studied in detail, the picture reveals a knife clenched in the right hand and a letter, "*Au Citoyen Marat*," in the left. After that, I often stole in to look at the picture, and the thought came to me : if the likeness be a faithful one, how strange that God should have molded in like form the personification of purity and gentleness and one who anticipated the vengeance of God as did Charlotte Corday.

THE NEW CUPID.

"'Tom." The champion pole vaulter of Yale.

"Harry." Since these lines were written, a famous athlete, and champion half-mile runner of America and France.

BALLADE OF A PLEASANT RECOLLECTION.

"We gay friends." M. S. B., H. A. W., Mabel and I.

JOHN BOYLE O'REILLY.

The seventh and eighth stanzas refer to the grand review of the Grand Army of the Republic, which took place in Boston, the second day after the gifted Irishman's sudden death at Hull.

BEAU BRUMMELL.

I thought, and still think, Mansfield's "Beau Brummell" one of the greatest creations of the modern stage.

SENATOR HOAR.

During the winter of 1890-91, the LI. Congress being then in its short session, I frequently went into the Senate Chamber to hear the debate upon the

Elections (called by its opponents the Force) Bill. Mr. Hoar, as chairman of the Committee on Privileges and Elections, conducted the debate for the Republican side, and I was often called upon to admire his patriotic replies to the attacks of his opponents. The bill failed to pass, but Mr. Hoar's eloquent and patriotic defence of the measure I shall never forget.

FATHER McGLYNN.

Though not endorsing his political ideas, I realized how honest and catholic a man he was.

THE PROUDEST NAME.

This was written in 1883, after Miss Howe's great success at the Worcester Festival, and before her return to Europe. She has always been loyal to America and to New England.

THE MARCH OF THE HEROES.

My father can bequeath to me no legacy more valued, no heritage more honorable, than the memory of his volunteer service in the armies of the Republic.

PINE GROVE SCHOOL.

"My children do no greater things." My dearly-beloved friend, M. S. B., so faithful in her work that she realized my ideal of the teacher who makes the district school "the corner-stone of the nation."

IN OLD SAINT JOHN'S.

The quaint old church, where Washington himself went, when he spent the Sabbath in the city, is always thronged with earnest worshippers. This was the vesper service, near the end of Lent.

MY MORNING WALK HOME.

In these days, when I was in the treadmill of a morning paper, I had a two-mile walk before me, when the paper had been "made up." With eyes aching from the glare of the incandescent lamps, brain weary and body fainting, I went down the narrow, dingy stairway, into the cool night, with a sense of relief and joy, and the long walk soothed me and put me in better humor with the world.

MY NEIGHBOR SWEET.

So many people go to our Festival that they may display their good clothes and be seen there !

This book has been printed, not for the many, but for One. Many of these rhymes I would not wish to preserve in a book issued to the general public, for no one realizes their literary short-comings more than I ; but for the sentiments ex-pressed I have no apologies to make. I have print-ed this little book with my own hands, from my own types, on my own press, at the request of the One for whom many of the verses it contains were directly written, and to whose gentle influence the others owe any nobility or strength of thought they may possess. It has been wholly a labor of love. The twenty copies issued are intended to reach only our immediate friends, but should some anti-quary, years hence, come upon a forgotten copy of this little book, let him find here no vaulting ambition in rhyme, but only the token of a pure and uplifting love and an unfaltering trust in God.

MABEL.